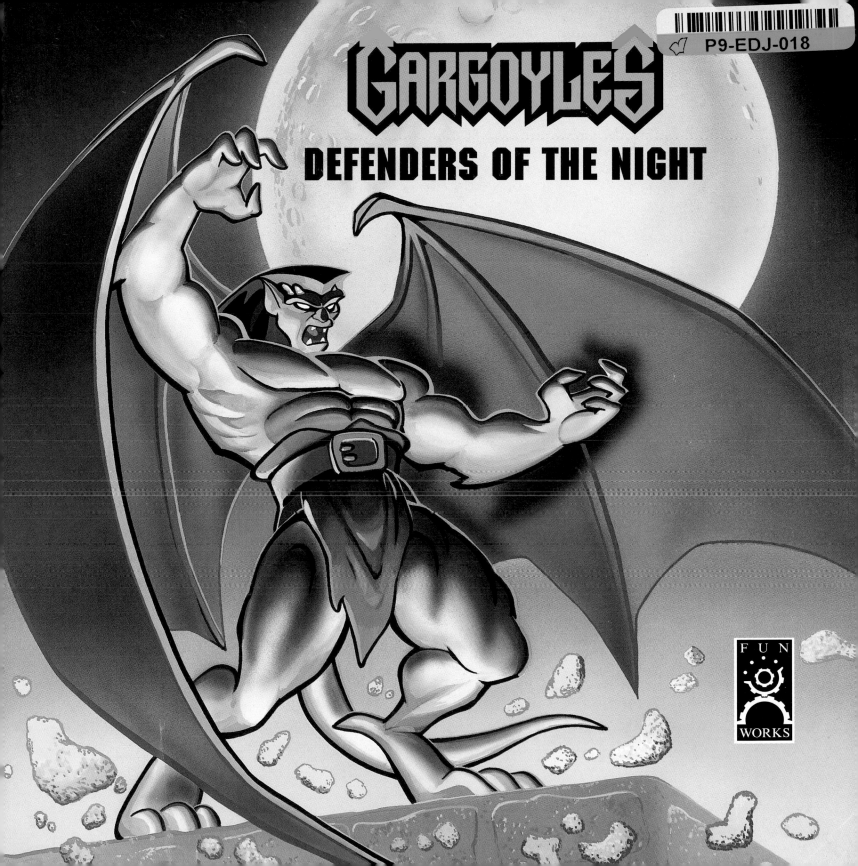

GARGOYLES
DEFENDERS OF THE NIGHT

P9-EDJ-018

FUN
WORKS

A thousand years ago, in the far-off mountains of Scotland, a young peasant boy named Tom watched from a tower as a band of fierce Viking warriors raided mysterious Castle Wyvern.

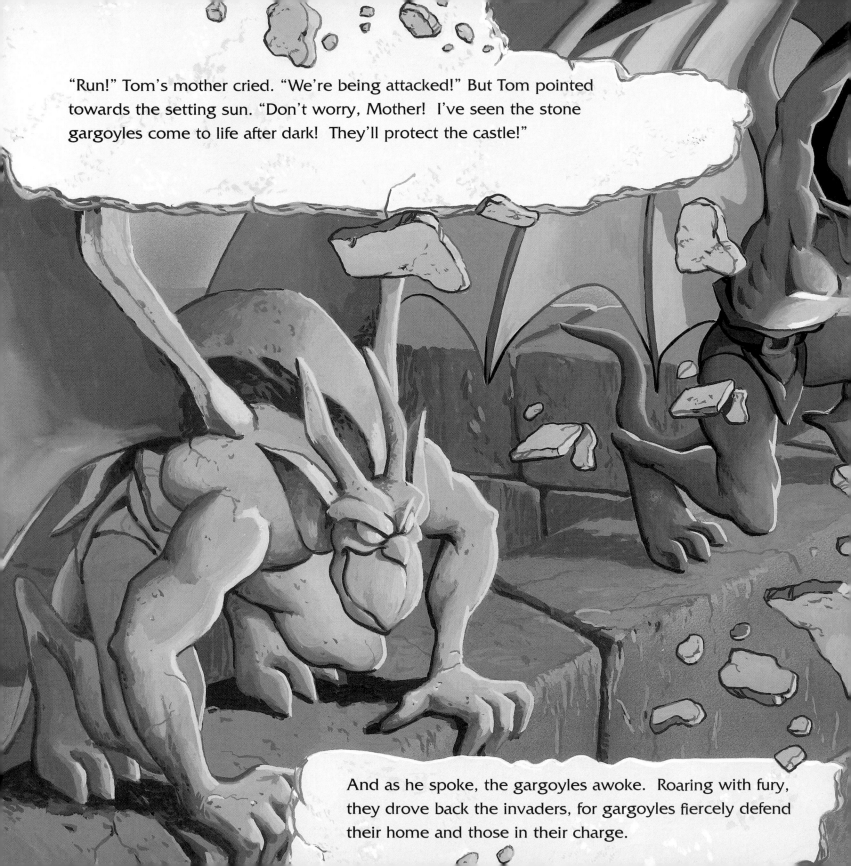

"Run!" Tom's mother cried. "We're being attacked!" But Tom pointed towards the setting sun. "Don't worry, Mother! I've seen the stone gargoyles come to life after dark! They'll protect the castle!"

And as he spoke, the gargoyles awoke. Roaring with fury, they drove back the invaders, for gargoyles fiercely defend their home and those in their charge.

Tom's mother was still afraid. "Gargoyles are just ugly beasts, Tom," she said. "They can hurt us as easily as the Vikings." Tom wished he could change his mother's fear. Just then, Goliath, the gargoyle leader, swooped by. "We would never hurt Castle Wyvern's people," he said. "We are your loyal defenders."

But other people feared the gargoyles as well, especially Princess Katharine and the Magus, her court magician. She refused to honor Goliath at the victory celebration. Instead of complaining, Goliath calmly left the room.

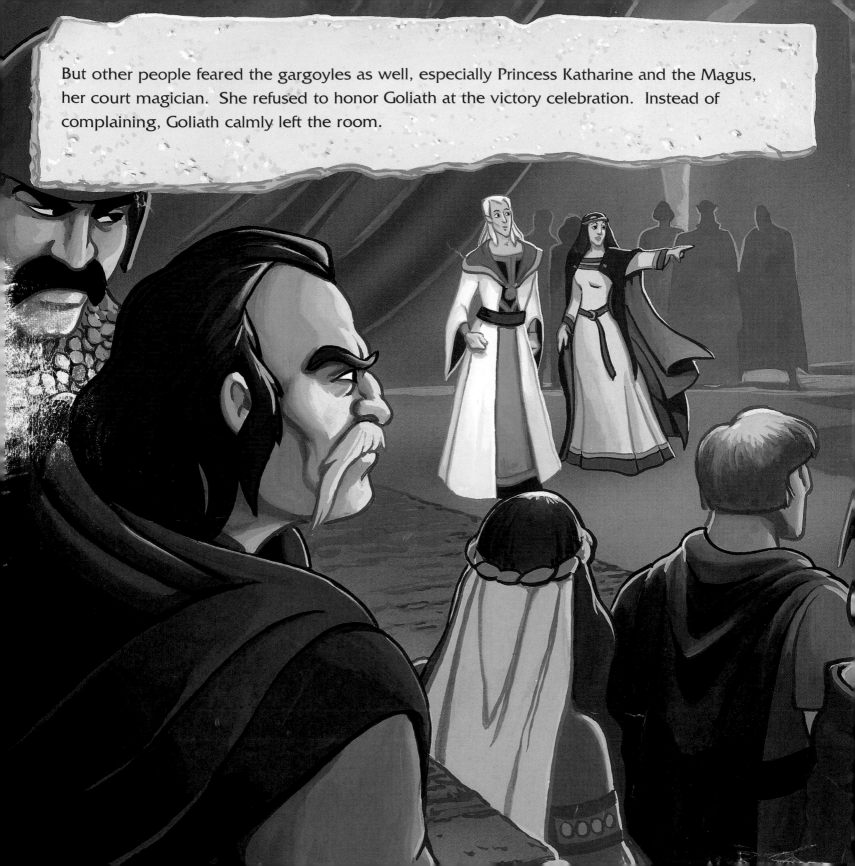

Goliath and his friends were sent away on a false mission. When they returned, they found that Castle Wyvern had been attacked by the Viking raiders. The gargoyles who had stayed behind had all been destroyed and the people taken captive. Goliath vowed to rescue the humans he had been sworn to protect.

The Vikings, with the help of Castle Wyvern's Captain of the Guard, had taken the prisoners to their mountain camp. It wasn't long before Goliath and his friends arrived and freed the captives. But Hakon, the Viking leader, and the Captain dragged Princess Katharine away before she could be rescued. Goliath flew after them to save her.

The Magus believed that the Princess had been killed because of the gargoyles' attack. In his rage, he cast a magic spell on Goliath's gargoyles to punish them: **"You will all sleep as stone until the castle rises above the clouds!"** he shouted. Horrified, Tom rushed to warn Goliath.

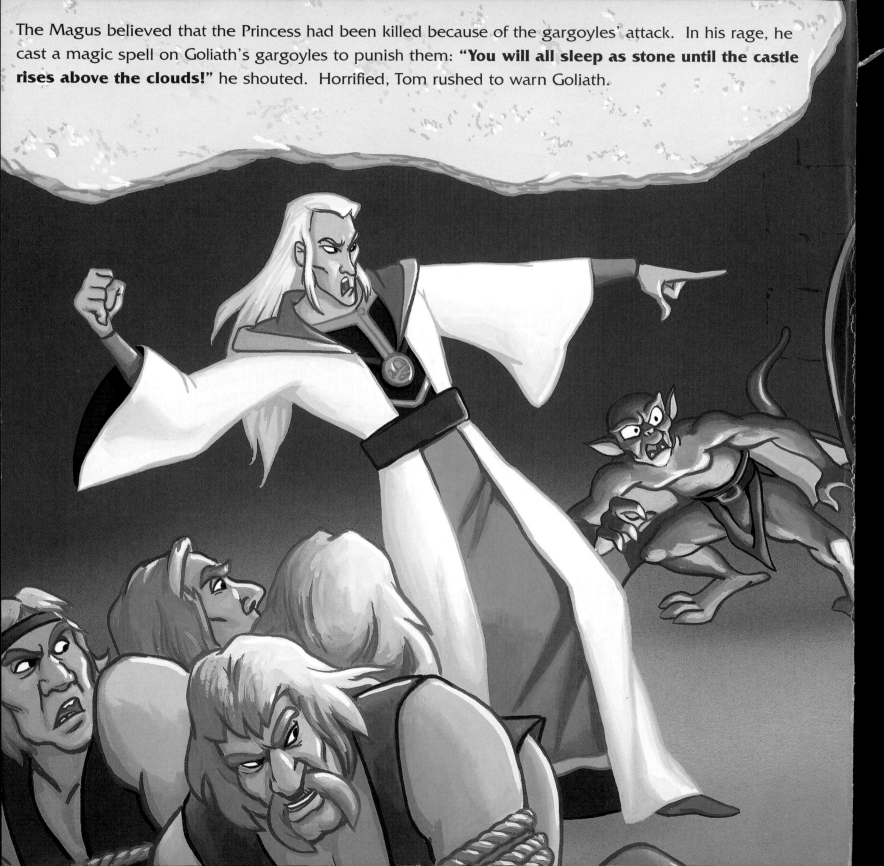

But Tom did not find Goliath. Instead, he saw the Captain fighting with Hakon while the Princess looked on in despair. Tom gasped as the struggling trio started to fall over a cliff.

Suddenly, Goliath swooped down from the sky and snatched the Princess in midair. The Captain and Hakon fell out of sight.

Goliath set the Princess safely down among her people. The Magus was torn between feeling relieved and ashamed. "Oh, Princess! I thought you were lost forever, so I enchanted the gargoyles!" he cried.

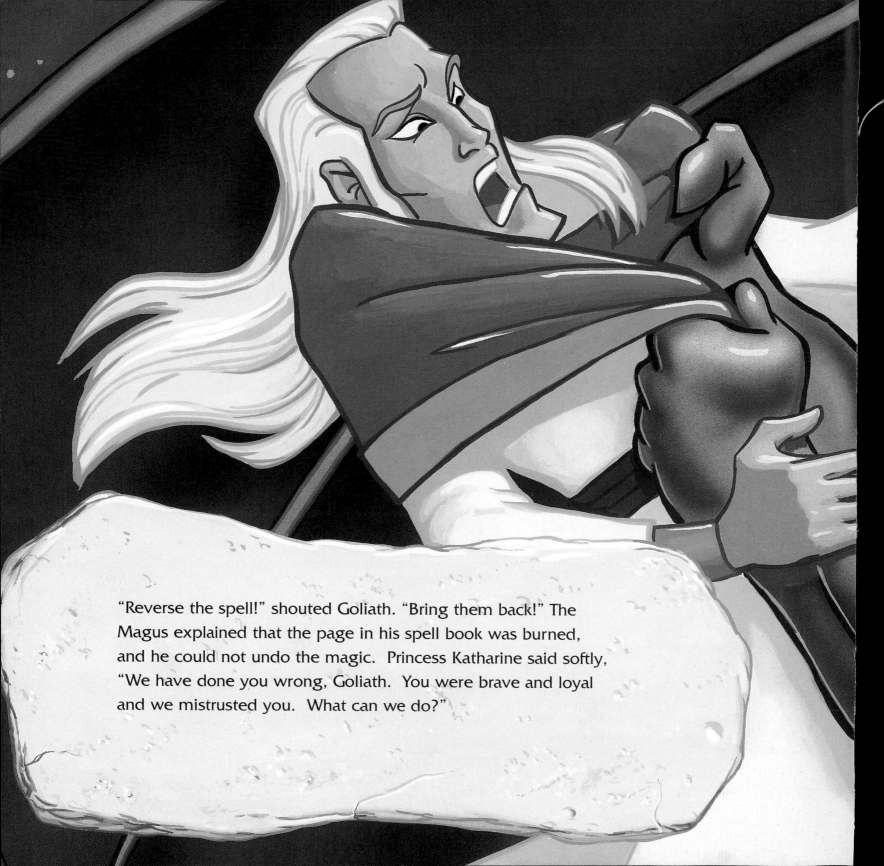

"Reverse the spell!" shouted Goliath. "Bring them back!" The Magus explained that the page in his spell book was burned, and he could not undo the magic. Princess Katharine said softly, "We have done you wrong, Goliath. You were brave and loyal and we mistrusted you. What can we do?"

Goliath thought for a moment and then beckoned to Tom. "The eggs in the Rookery will soon hatch. They will need guidance," Goliath explained. "Help Tom care for our eggs."

Goliath took a deep breath. He knew there was nothing else to be done. "But first, Magus, cast your spell one more time, so I can join my friends."

And so Goliath was turned to stone like the other gargoyles, to wait out the long years. Filled with pride at his new responsibility, Tom looked up at his enchanted heroes hoping that he would someday be as brave and loyal as these mighty defenders of the night.